THE NEW WORLD

CHRISTIAN D. CHU

Content

Prologue

It all began in 2050. The year my brother and I were born. I never had parents. They ditched us when we were young, and honestly, I can't blame them. It was hard enough for a couple to survive, let alone a couple with kids. The world was over once the nuclear war started.

Countries were deleted in the blink of an eye, and in the first few years, a hundred or so countries were destroyed. The nuclear war laid waste to the Earth, and toxic chemicals spread everywhere. The air was so polluted that people struggled to breathe.

This was when everything changed. Somehow, the chemicals affected us infants differently. We gained special abilities, based on the conditions of how we lived. Some kids didn't get affected by the chemicals, but I did. I didn't have to breathe in oxygen to survive, and I could absorb the air around me. When I did, I would get stronger and faster. My brother, however, didn't get any powers. This post-apocalyptic world was dangerous. Governments had been overthrown long ago. Now, gangs run our world.

●

My dreams haunt me, reminding me of my worst nightmares. They repeat, night after night, over and over, until they take over me. Losing my friends, watching kids like me die. The one that stays with me the most is the loss of my brother.

I can still hear the footsteps following us in the rain. The shouts that echo within the streets. My heart hammering in my chest, I remember sprinting away from the noise, away from trouble. Using all the strength I can muster, I take in the air around me, more than ever before, leaving none for my pursuers. Hearing them cough and gasp for air puts a smile on my face, if not just for a few seconds, before I hear a crash to my right. In horror, I realize it's my brother, Casper, who tripped and fell face flat on the pavement. In my head, I'm screaming at him to get up, but it is already too late. My sudden hesitation allows the air in the room to flow out of me.

In that sudden moment of fear, my mind blanks. I feel at a sudden loss, and I can't summon my powers. Frantically, I try to suck in all the oxygen again, but it's too late. The pursuers catch their breath and reach my brother. My brain tells me to stay and fight, but the rest of me wants to run away. Tears pouring down my face, I sprint away, leaving behind the last remnants of my family, and my best friend.

All I can think about is how it was my fault that my brother was gone. They were after my power. They saw me use it on a gangster trying to rob us. I didn't know what they did to my brother, but I knew it wasn't good.

Even to this day, I hear Casper's screams travel throughout the night sky, even after the nightmares stop and I wake up. Casper haunts me, and regret fills me to the bone. As time goes on, my regret and remorse morph into anger. My body burns with rage, vengeance coursing through my veins.

I will make them pay. They will feel my revenge. They will fear me. I will do anything to stop future kids like me from watching their families get ripped from them. As I get out of my bed, and look out below me, I see how much I accomplished. Everything I created, every single person I recruited for the Liberti Warriors, was for Casper.

When I was Darian, I didn't have the power to protect Casper. Now, I do. I am the leader of the Liberti Warriors. I am Airless.

Chapter. 1

Hope

"Be quiet, sis. They're coming," My brother whispers to me as he peeks through the small cracks in the wall. I suck in a breath as fear creeps up my spine, causing me to stay on edge. My brother crawls back into our little makeshift home, trying to hide from the gang. People have always wondered what it would be like to live in an apocalypse. My brother and I, along with a few others left in our town, have experienced it firsthand. Gangs own the streets, and every day they find one survivor to torment. We've learned to hide. I am special, though.

Ever since I was young, I felt different. Maybe this was because I had the ability to breathe underwater. Suddenly, we hear a shriek come from outside. I shuffle forwards and peek through the cracks. I feel my heart drop as I notice it's my friend, Jane.

She's being dragged out into the daylight by her hair, and the gang members are laughing. My brother pulls me back and drags me back into our dark, hobbit-like hole. We sit there and wait. We wait until there are no more screams, until we hear them leave.

"Nye, we can't just wait here. You know how close they were to finding us. Jane was practically our neighbor!" I shout at Nye once I know the gang is not in earshot.

"I know, Hope, but where are we going to move? It took us days just to find this place, and we were almost caught by the gang near the broken bridge." As a ray of sunlight shines through, I can see the wrinkles on his face. Stress has not been good for him.

Just then, I hear someone muttering from the streets, and I instantly recognize that voice. Anyone living in what used to be the US knows or has heard about the person with that voice. It's Panther, one of the most prominent and well-known members of the Crimson Powers. If he's here, that means the other gang members are not far behind. My heart rate quickens, reaching almost double its original speed, as I wonder why they are here when their headquarters are around 30 kilometers away from here, in the Oregon scavenger pits. As time ticks by, I can hear voices getting closer and closer. My brother and I pray that Panther and his thugs get nowhere close to us. However, the sounds get louder until we can hear what they're saying, word for word. I can hear their footsteps, and it's not until a full thirty or so minutes that we breathe a sigh of relief.

Our day ends there as the last few rays of sunshine disappear, the day already fading away. I curl into a fetal position, and let my dreams drift me to sleep before something grabs a hold of me and covers my mouth. I struggle and shout as I see my kidnapper, Panther, and his thugs surround my brother. Nye is struggling to keep them back, with both arms held up to intimidate the gang, although I know it's no use. My brother is even weaker than I am and has never engaged in a fight.

Surprisingly, though, the Crimson Powers are not engaging, and stand in a circle around him. Suddenly, I can feel something icy and sharp drag slowly across my neck. My brother sees it as well. A knife.

"Put your hands up, or this girl gets it!" I can hear the person who is grabbing me warn my brother. At this moment, I can feel his grip loosen on me, and I take advantage. Kicking at the kidnapper, I hear him grunt and I immediately rip my arms free. I can hear other shouts and grunts as both of us manage to escape with the element of surprise on our side.

Afraid of turning back, I run as fast as I can, using my knowledge of the area to get out of the ruined building. I land on the floor just as I feel something crack. I look down, and my leg pops out to the side. Just looking at my leg makes me wince.

"Help," I groan to my brother, who has already started running off into the distance. Seeing the condition of my leg, his face starts to pale. He runs back and tries to carry me away, but to no avail. We already know we aren't going to make it, with me unable to walk, and the gang members streaming out of the building.

Putting our heads down in defeat, we are about to say our goodbyes when I notice something. Just to the left of the building, I can barely make out a hooded figure, dressed in black that blends in perfectly with the shadows. If it wasn't for the person's movements, I wouldn't have seen him anyways. Peering closely, I see a small medal-looking thing glint in the darkness. Just then, I hear a voice.

"You two shouldn't have run. We weren't here to hurt both of you. We just want you." At this, Panther points at me, and up close I can see why he got his nickname. His face is curled into a natural snarl, with two teeth jutting out of his mouth, like fangs. His dark, black hair covers most of his face, and his narrowed eyes glare at us through his mass of hair.

"Get away from us, please. We didn't do anything wrong." My brother tries to reason with them, but they don't listen. Instead, one of the gang members grab my brother by the head and punch him in the face. Immediately, I am up on my feet, rushing towards my brother, but someone gets there before me. The person zooms through the gang members, sending groups of them falling to the floor. He turns to face Panther, and that's when I see his face. A teenage boy, maybe sixteen, stands in front of the gang members. Surprisingly, he has no fear reflected on his face. He stares down the gang members as dissent spreads through the Crimson Powers.

"Go away, child. You better leave before we make you." Panther shouts, but the words don't seem to affect the teen. Suddenly, the mysterious figure opens his mouth.

"Leave these children alone. They're now under the protection of the Liberti Warriors." The medal I saw before glints under the lamplight, and I realize what it is: A Warrior medal.

Chapter. 2

Panther and a few other bold members of the Crimson Powers scoffed at his words, but many more were starting to look wary. Everyone has heard of the Liberti Warriors: an elite group of teens who have special abilities that are trying to save others like them. Their achievements were legendary.

Since their creation in 2058, they have added warrior after warrior to their ranks. Everyone heard of Airless, the founder of the group who single-handedly took down one of the biggest gangs in the United States. Another well-known member was Lightwave, supposedly the first member of the Liberti Warriors, and recruited at age 5. Just the thought of Lightwave being invisible stopped most of the small gangs from ever committing crimes.

Gang members and people alike were shocked when one of the oldest members, Nova, who had the power to control explosions, died in combat against the Dreads. Since then, Airless made it his personal mission to end the gang, and has slaughtered every single one of the Dreads, exterminating them in a matter of days. No one has heard of the gang for 8 years. I think about this moment, and the rumors about Airless. Wasn't this a bit overboard? Were the Liberti Warriors actually doing the right thing?

At the thought, I realized that he was here for me. To recruit me. One look at my brother tells me he thought the exact same thing. Why would they want me? I thought to myself, eyebrows furrowed. I wasn't a warrior like them. I could only breathe underwater, which was a pretty useless skill in a battle. Maybe they wanted me as a spy?

As I was thinking, it led me to another thought. What if he was only here to save me? What if he separated my brother and I? My heart starts to hammer in my chest, realizing that I might be taken away from the last remnants of my family.

I am snapped back to reality as the shouts and screams from the Crimson Powers grow louder. Panther and a few of his goons are charging at the boy, metal pipes and rusted knives in hand. I stared as he sprinted towards them, mouth curled upwards in a grin. His hands brushed past the gang members, one by one, and sizzling sounds filled the room. Wherever he touched left a huge burn mark on his victims. Suddenly, I remembered. I had heard of a Warrior who was known to have recruited some of the best, and that he went by Charcoal. His power both fascinated and horrified me. He must be a heavy hitter for the Liberti Warriors. There was no chance that I would be able to hurt people with such little remorse or guilt.

At this point, all hell broke loose. Gang members were running left and right, while more were clutching their burn marks and getting knocked out at the hands of Charcoal.

Panther stood there amidst it all, as shocked as we were. Finally, he rushed at us, hoping to escape amidst the chaos with us in hand, but it seemed as if Charcoal had his eyes on Panther. In the blink of an eye, Charcoal appeared in front of us, blocking his way. Panther screamed as Charcoal grabbed onto his face, scorching it and leaving huge scars. We watched in horror as smoke started to emerge from Panther's face, as Charcoal stood there with a blank face. The smell of burnt flesh filled the air, and the sizzling sound from the fire was getting louder, causing both of us to choke and gag.

The smoke was spreading like a wildfire, blocking my vision. Everything became hazy, and I was only mildly aware that I had fallen to my feet, coughing. It was getting harder and harder for me to breathe. Suddenly, I felt someone lift me to my feet. As my eyes focused, I realized it was my brother. The screams and shouts from Panther attracted my attention. Charcoal was still slamming his fist into Panther's face, punch after punch, as if it was personal.

Panther's face was unrecognizable now. His once distinct face was now bloody and swollen.

Finally, I couldn't take it anymore. "Stop!" I yelled at Charcoal, not wanting someone to die at my expense. Surprisingly, Charcoal obliged, letting go of Panther's face and pushing him to the ground. His eyes glowed a dark red, and he looked at me for a split second, before looking away. I was startled at the color of his eyes. Was that normal?

"Follow me," Charcoal commanded us, not giving us any time to process what we just saw.

"What just happ-" My brother's question was cut off abruptly as Charcoal turned around and glared at him: "Just follow me. We'll explain it all later." I could see my brother start to open his mouth, probably asking about who Charcoal was referring to. I shoved him hard enough for him to look back at me, and gave him a withering look, shutting him up.

Not wanting to get on the bad side of Charcoal, I decided to follow him as he navigated us through the carcass of San Francisco, the sun just rising over the horizon. My brother hurried along, his feet shuffling across the dried-up land.

As we walked towards the light, I knew nothing would be the same. Leaving the shouts and chaos of the remaining Crimson Gang members, I walked into the distance, leaving my old life behind.

Chapter. 3

We trudged alongside the remains of a road until we stumbled across an abandoned warehouse. There were bits and pieces of the warehouse strewn across the floor, and chunks of the wall were missing, leaving a large, gaping hole in its place.

I raised an eye and signaled my brother, who just shrugged and continued walking. Since no one had talked for what felt like an eternity, I decided to break the ice.

"So Charcoal, what's your story?" I asked him, hoping for a reply. Unsurprisingly, he just continued walking as if he hadn't heard my question. "Are you sure this is the right place?" I asked again, hoping for at least a reply.

"Yes, I'm sure. Now shut up," Charcoal grumbled as he walked into the warehouse. I followed him until we reached a stone wall. It was in horrible condition, with multiple dents and cracks in the grayish concrete wall. I opened my mouth to ask Charcoal what we were doing here, when he pressed a slightly lighter-colored brick. At once, the brick wall split in two, leaving a decorated corridor. I stifled a gasp, which made Charcoal smirk.

"Follow me," he said for about the fifth time. Excitement coursed through my veins. This is where the Liberti Warriors lived! I quickened my pace to match Charcoal, eager to finally meet the legendary heroes. However, when we turned the corner, I was disappointed, to say the least.

Instead of warriors like Airless and Lightwave, all I could see were a bunch of teens around my age. Before I could look around, Charcoal dragged me over to the teens who seemed like they were training.

"Introduce yourselves," stated Charcoal, his voice echoing throughout the room.

One of the teens who had bright pink hair approached my brother first. "Hey guys, the name's Echo. My power is that I can control people for a short time, and I'm 12 this year." She spoke extremely fast to the point where I could barely comprehend what she was saying. At first glance, I was surprised at how this girl is only 12, considering she looked much older. Then, I noticed the tattoo on the side of her arm.

"What's that?" I point at it, but Echo's smile immediately disappears, replaced with an expressionless face. "That was from my old life."

Charcoal started to speak again, and I turned to look at him.

"This is Void," he says, pointing at a girl with black hair and black clothes, "she doesn't really talk to anyone, but she is 13 this year, and she has the ability to influence other people's emotions." I wave at her, but she doesn't respond. She just stares back at me blankly, causing me to shiver.

"Don't worry, she's like that to everyone." Echo walks closer to me, rolling her eyes. "What's your name, by the way?"

I am taken aback at the bluntness of Echo, but I quickly manage a response. "I'm Hope. This is my brother Nye. I can breathe underwater."

"So, what's your brother's ability?" Echo asks, eyebrows raised.

"He doesn't really have any superpowers," I responded meekly. At these words, Echo gasps.

"We've never had a non-super in the training facility before!" She shouts, her voice raising an octave higher than normal.

At this, Charcoal jumps in. "We will give hospitality to Hope's brother for now. But thanks for reminding me, Echo. Hope, I expect you to begin your training very soon." Charcoal raises his hand and immediately, two men come in, whisking my brother off. Then, he motions for me to follow.

Charcoal leads me deeper into the compound. Looking

around, I can see many of them are roughly my age. I was so busy taking in the surroundings that I didn't hear what Charcoal was saying.

"Excuse me?" I respond, not knowing what else to say.

"I asked you if you were ready to start training today." He muttered something, then looked at me, waiting for my response.

"Yeah, sure," I replied. In all honesty, I was really looking forward to honing and mastering my ability. However, what came next wasn't what I expected.

Charcoal called over Echo and Void to join me. He then started to pace across the room, speaking in a teacher-like voice. "As you guys know, we have a new student among us. However, Hope, you will be expected to try your hardest to keep up with the others. Now, we will begin with our normal warm-up, consisting of stamina and strength exercises. Afterwards, we will focus on honing our special abilities."

Echo and Void proceed to the running track immediately. I follow them, unsure about my stamina. In a matter of minutes, I get proof that my earlier wariness was correct. While the other two trainees were running around the track with no clear indication of stopping, I was already doubled over, and gasping for air.

I hear footsteps behind me, and I whirl around to see

Charcoal glancing disapprovingly. "Get up," he commands, and I do, wheezing all the while. "If you want to be a Liberti Warrior, you've got a long way to go." I bite my lip to stop me from talking back, although anger courses through me. This was my first day. How would I be as good as the others?

"Run," Charcoal commands, but I can't continue.

"Can I just catch my breath for a bit?" I ask him, although I already kind of know the answer.

"No, run," he replies, getting more aggravated by the second. I curse Charcoal a bit too loudly, and for a second, I'm scared he heard me. However, he walks away, and I breathe a sigh of relief, until I remember that I must continue running. How is this only the warmup? I trudge along, starting to worry if I really am Warrior material.

Chapter. 4

Hours passed. Days blurred together. I could feel the differences in my strength and speed. When I used to only be able to run for 10 minutes, I managed to double that in just 3 days. My strength increased twofold as well. However, my improvements didn't mean much to Charcoal. He still constantly lectured and scolded me for being lazy, or not giving my all. At this point, I couldn't care less.

Another major upgrade was that I was getting closer to some of the other trainees. Echo and I bonded on the second day after we both sulked at Charcoal's orders. From then on, we became good friends.

I could now slightly keep up with the others. The feeling as power coursed through me, if not just for a few seconds, exhilarated me. The only thing I struggled with was honing my abilities.

It seems like no matter how many times I try to focus, my powers waver and it leads to me gasping for air and resurfacing.

However, I was not the only one who struggled at this part. Echo could never use her powers correctly. Once, she was supposed to control Void, but ended up controlling Charcoal, who went stricter on her. I felt bad for her, but I was still busy focusing on my own powers that I couldn't do much except sympathize.

As the day ended, us trainees headed back to the dorm rooms. I zoned out as Echo started complaining about Charcoal, thinking about the friends and people I ditched from my old life. At this thought, I realized I hadn't seen my brother since we first came here. Where was he?

"-Charcoal annoying?" As I came back to my senses, I heard part of Echo's sentence. I didn't bother to answer, instead asking a question of my own.

"Guys, do you know where my brother is?" Both shake their heads no.

"Maybe he's living in one of the staff's rooms?" Echo suggests, but I knew that was not the case. Other than Charcoal and some bodyguards, I knew of no "staff" in this hideout.

"I'll go look for him," I answered, and proceeded to walk out the door, not listening to their protests.

Walking down the corridor connecting the trainee rooms and the facility, I wandered around until I noticed another hall which I've never been to before. As I looked to my left and right, I noticed no one there. The skin on my arms pricked up as I realized the trouble I was going to get into if I were caught, and my feet turned weak.

Just as I'm about to turn back, I stumble across multiple solid metal doors, with a small window on each one. They look like doors that cage dangerous prisoners, which piques my interest. Approaching the first door, I get on my tiptoes to look into the closest glass window.

At first, I see nothing, then something pops into view, and I jerk back, desperately holding my scream. Inside, there stands a person covered in scales, each scale piercing through the person's own skin. Even the person's face has multiple protruding spikes, making him look like a mutated porcupine.

The person stares at me and starts to scream, his voice echoing throughout the corridor. All around, people start showing their faces through the window. They scream and shout, their voices becoming one. The only similarity all of them have is that they all look messed up, some with thorns protruding out of their bodies, others with missing eyes and noses.

Just then, in the corner of my eye, I can see someone speeding towards me. Charcoal. His hand emits a burst of fire, and his eyes glow dark red, quieting all the people at once.

"What are you doing here?" Charcoal yells once no sound is to be heard and we move away from the mutated people. His hands are closed into fists, each holding fire. His red eyes are glowing with anger, just like when I saw him fight against Panther.

"I-I'm sorry. I was just looking for my brother and I thought he was here." I reply meekly. For a second, I thought that Charcoal would burn me right here right now. However, he just looks down, as if expecting that I would have asked this.

"I'm sorry Hope," he replies in a whisper, so soft that I almost don't hear him. "He wandered off a few nights ago. I tried to warn him, but he didn't listen. The Crimson Powers got him."

Without realizing, my eyes turn to slits. I can feel my heart beating out of my chest, my palms balled into fists. I am no longer scared of Charcoal. Suddenly, my heart aches, and I fall to the ground clutching my chest. Something's familiar about this feeling, though. Just then, I feel a pulse, then two, then three. I look down at my hand and I am surprised to see it glow translucent with a hint of blue.

I shout in surprise, causing my brain to throb. My head falls back, and I shout, my voice echoing throughout the silent corridor. In the back of my head, Charcoal's voice drifts in, but it's growing quieter by the second. I can only hear the last sentence he says: "Hope, your powers."

All of a sudden, the pain stops. I stand up, confused as my brain tries to process what just happened. I was in a corridor, and

Charcoal came. What else? Shaking my head, I try to recall why I was on the floor. In the corner of my eye stands Charcoal, his eyes wide and unblinking, staring straight back at me.

"What?" I exclaimed, confused and still shaking that weird feeling from my head.

Charcoal just stares at me and points, his mouth widening. I look down and instead of my usual human torso, I see a translucent blob of water, floating around. A second glance tells me my whole body has changed.

"Oh," I trembled, voice faltering. My head starts to hurt, my chest starts to ache, and I fall to my knees, shouting. The last thing I can see is a burst of bright light, as everything turns black.

Chapter. 5

Nye

"Wake up," a voice from afar, spreading through my brain. Another shout, a push, and my eyelids split apart. A face comes into view, although I don't recognize him immediately. Scars cover his face, and there is a massive burnt handprint on his face: Panther.

I immediately flinch away, finally taking in my surroundings. It's extremely dark and I can see trash littered everywhere. Surrounding me are around ten others, all with the logo that signifies them as part of the Crimson Powers. Some are smirking, but all have the marks from the last brutal encounter with Charcoal.

"It's fine, kid. We won't hurt you," Panther assures, although some others grimace at these words. "We're here to tell you the truth. Follow us." He extends his hand to help me up, but before I can even comprehend what's going on, sparks start appearing from the nearby streetlights. It flickers, on and off, before suddenly bursting to flames.

For a minute, I thought it was Charcoal, but this was different. From the lights emerge a figure surrounded by sparks; his body made up of tiny electric tendrils. At once, the street is filled with pandemonium.

"Hurry up, kid, they're here!" Panther shouts over the commotion and pulls me as he and some others start running.

"What is going on?" I yell over the crowd. I turn my head back and catch a glimpse of Cypher, another Warrior, approaching, surrounded by a mystical aura. Screams fill the night as I follow Panther through multiple alleys, turning left and right.

Sparks continue to fly all around us, and a sudden boom propels me forwards. My head burns and I struggle to get up as Cypher approaches.

Suddenly, a man with a single large scar across his face steps in between the pulsating Cypher and me. His face surprisingly shows no fear, and he proceeds to flick his wrists. In a flash, manholes leading to the sewer are blasted into the air, as jets upon jets of water are blasted at Cypher. Cypher pulls back in shock and jumps right back into an unbroken lightbulb. Flickers of electricity spark in the air before it disappears down the street.

I stare in shock as I try to process what I just witnessed. I turn to stare at the man, who can't be younger than 30. He grins and extends a hand, helping me to my feet.

"How...?" I am stunned into silence, and the mysterious man just laughs. At this, Panther comes into view, smiling and embracing the man who just saved my life.

"Nye, this here is Jonas. We met a few years back. Don't worry, he's a fine man. He won't hurt you." Panther walks to me and looks Jonas straight in the eye, talking in whispers. At this point, I can only manage to hear a few words, but it doesn't tell me much.

After a few awkward minutes of them talking, Jonas turns to me with a smile on his face. "I bet you were wondering how I got these sick powers, right, kid? Well, the Crimson Powers have finally managed to transfer these powers. I was the first customer." He grins again, but what he said haunts me. What if they do this to my sister?

"What did you do to the kid?" I yell, and even I am taken aback for a moment at how angry I sound. I jerked back from Panther and Jonas, suddenly conscious that I was hanging around gangsters who almost hurt my sister and I. This was when I realized my sister wasn't here. Where was she?

Before I could figure out an answer to the question, Panther spoke. "Don't worry, we didn't harm the previous owner of Jonas's power. We weren't trying to harm your sister either." I glared at him, staying a few feet away.

"Stay back!" I yelled, "How'd you find me?" I looked desperately to find something to defend myself with, but there was nothing around me.

"The Warriors are bad, Nye. Trust me, they are not as good as they seem." Panther looked so serious, and his eyes seemed to bore into my soul. I thought it was wise not to argue.

"We're going to take you to one of our hideouts, and make sure it's a safe space before we tell you the whole story." I tried to refuse, but looking at my odds of escaping, they were pretty grim. All I could do was agree. Although I convinced myself that the Warriors were good, there was still some part of me that was curious what they meant. I nodded slowly, hesitating when they motioned for me to follow.

At my nod, Charcoal and Jonas head off with me in tow, sneaking through multiple alleys and groups of people. As we walk, Jonas starts to ask me some questions: "So, Nye, what can your sister do? I heard she has powers relating to water, like me."

I didn't know what to reply, so I just nodded. "Awkward," chuckles Jonas as we walk.

As we walked, the silence was thick as ice, so I decided to ask a question of my own: "Jonas, where did you come from?" He just looked back and sneered, as if saying "You don't want to know". "Ok, chill," I mutter, looking back down.

In the corner of my eye, I can see Panther passing some sort of message to some other Crimson gang members. I only make out the words "Cypher" and "kill". Hearing this makes my heart beat out of my chest, and I am much more wary of hearing the "truth" from Panther. What if they just brought me there to kill me?

My head hurt at the multiple questions left unanswered. However, just as I was pondering, we approached two others guarding what looked like a club.

"It's us, tell the boss." Panther motions at the two men, but they glance at me and shake their heads.

"Who the hell is that? Stragglers are not allowed here, scram!" The first person yells at me, motioning for me to leave. However, Panther and Jonas stand their ground.

"He's with us, Leo. Don't forget who gave you those powers." Panther sneers, and I realize that this guy, Leo, is clutching a ball of fire, completely unharmed.

Leo looks wary, looking back at me, then at Panther. Finally, he heaves a sigh and opens the door, allowing us to pass.

We walk in, seeing bunches of people dancing to the music. I walk around in disbelief, not knowing places like this still existed. Every square inch is packed, and it takes us forever to walk through the crowd, finally reaching a man who had bodyguards to his left and right. He looked really familiar, with his hair cut like a mohawk.

"Who's this?" I whisper to Jonas, but Panther is the one who responds.

"Nye, let me introduce you to my close friend, a person who is a close ally of the Crimson Powers." Panther begins, but he does not get to finish.

"Panther, I can introduce myself." He jokes, then extends his hand, reaching for a handshake. "Hey Nye, my name is Casper. You might know my brother, Airless."

Chapter. 6

For a second there, I couldn't comprehend what the man just said. Airless, the legendary Liberti Warrior, had a brother? And his brother worked for the Crimson Powers? How? Why? I just stared in disbelief, trying to take everything in. Luckily, Casper spoke before I could ask any more questions.

"I'm guessing you brought him here for me to tell him the truth?" Casper raises his eyebrows at Panther, who just shrugs and nods. "Well, the truth is this, Nye. I'm the reason that Airless, or Darian, started the Liberti Warriors." At this, I try to ask a question, but I am immediately silenced by Jonas, while Casper continues.

"When we were young, our parents were killed at a very young age, leaving my brother and I to fend for ourselves. One day, the leader of another gang found out that my brother had exceptional abilities and tried to capture us. I was caught, but my brother managed to get away. However, the Crimson Powers, who were then led by Panther's father, managed to save me. They have cared for me since."

When he says this, I'm confused. "Why don't you just tell the people the truth? We all think you're trying to hurt us!" I shout, partly because I thought it was outrageous, but mainly because I believed the Liberti Warriors myself.

Jonas is about to shush me once more, but Casper holds up his hand. "It's fine," he says, then looks me straight in the eye. "Nye, I wanted to tell people, especially my brother, that I was alive, but he didn't believe me. He has already put too much into the Liberti Warriors, so much so that he forgot what he was originally trying to accomplish." Casper then pulls down part of his shirt collar, revealing a scar etched onto his skin, similar to Panther's scars from Charcoal. "He sent Charcoal to do this to me the moment I saw him. I tried to talk, but he didn't listen. He didn't believe I was alive. From then on, I knew my brother was gone." Casper's eyes welled up with tears, holding back the heartbreak.

In a matter of seconds, the tears are gone, replaced with a pure look of resolve. Casper then proceeds to continue: "The Crimson Powers aren't as bad as you think they are. They transfer these powers to adults who are capable of handling them, saving these kids from other gangs looking to harness these abilities. The reason we brought you here was because we're worried that the Warriors are getting too powerful. They have warrior after warrior, trained to harness their abilities and kill with no mercy. You saw what they could do: Cypher, Charcoal, Airless, Lightwave, and now Stinger and Anesthesia. We need help, and we know you will do anything to save your sister from getting brainwashed. We know you will help us."

My brain is still comprehending the things I've heard, and I'm wary that they are telling the truth, but the more they talk the more I believe them. Honestly, I never really bought the Warriors' act. However, I decided to test them a bit further. "At least the Liberti Warriors aren't snatching children off the streets, which is exactly what you guys are doing." I say, although with less confidence.

Panther looks at Casper then, and I know something's wrong. Casper motions for me to follow him and we walk into a small, locked room. The small room looks as if it were fifty years old, paint peeling everywhere, but that's not what catches my attention. In the middle of the room holds three body bags, all with fresh blood leaking through.

I look in horror, but before I can freak out, Jonas steps in. "Don't worry, we didn't kill these children. The Warriors did." I'm shocked at this statement, considering I never heard of them massacring kids, only recruiting them.

Someone suddenly puts their hand on my shoulder, and I jerk around to see Casper, a solemn look on his face. "The Liberti

Warriors are very secretive. They don't want their secrets leaking out, so when trainees fail or don't pass, they execute them. We found these bodies lying in the street," Casper states, looking uncomfortable.

"So how come you know the Liberti Warriors killed them?" I wonder, until Jonas opens the body bags. Two of the bodies have multiple burn wounds, all looking like it came from Charcoal. The final body is scarred beyond recognition, electricity still zipping around the body. Charcoal and Cypher.

I feel as if my heart is crumbling, cracking open from all the lies that were fed to me. Why would they do that? What if this happened to my sister? The sight before me strengthened my resolve. I knew I would do anything I could to bring back my sister, to save him from these cold-blooded murderers.

"So, what do you want me to do?" I ask, thirsty for revenge, anger towards the Warriors and their lies flooding through my body.

Casper looks at Panther, and Panther nods once. Then, Casper looks at me, smiling. "Follow me," he mouths over the noise, and along with Panther, we walk deeper into the building, finally reaching a large door.

Surprisingly, the room behind the door is fancy and new, looking like one of those science laboratories in movies. Right as we walk in, there are multiple men and women in lab coats hurrying around, shouting random things I don't understand.

Casper stops in front of a child who's holding a small teddy bear. The child suddenly teleports a few feet away. I stare, shell-shocked, never seeing someone who could teleport. Casper says something, and I turn to look. He's smiling, but I don't know what he asked me.

Embarrassed, I asked him to repeat what he said. He smiles again, and so does Panther. This time when he speaks, his voice rings loud and clear, echoing throughout the room and causing all the people to raise their heads. "Nye, how would you like some powers of your own?"

Chapter. 7

When I wake up, there are three people standing around me. It takes me a minute to remember what happened before I fainted, but when I do, I feel like fainting all over again. "Are you guys serious?" I reply, awestruck. Although my sister had powers, I never thought of what it would be like for me to have my own, especially a power as cool as teleportation.

Panther nods, smirking. He walks over to me and looks me up and down. "You've got what it takes. I know it," he insisted, and Jonas and Casper were both nodding as well.

I start to get excited and ask Panther a few questions regarding my new powers. However, I'm interrupted. Casper has a stern look on his face, showing he means business. "Don't think that these powers come without a cost. We're trusting that you put your heart and soul into training, and that you help our cause." I am so thrilled that I vigorously nod, but I also started to think. Why did the Crimson Powers seem so similar to the Liberti Warriors, training people to fight for their cause?

Before I started to be wary of Panther and his gang, they called me over. "So, you ready kid?" Panther questioned. "This can't be reversed, so this is your only chance to back out. This power would put you in danger, but it would also make you stronger, more capable. Do you accept this power?" It doesn't even take me a second to say yes, eager to try out my new abilities.

"Ok, Nye, follow us. We'll take you to the operating table. While you're there, try to stay still." I follow them into yet another room, this one with even more people walking around in lab coats. Two people wearing lab coats approach us, and I recognize one. Jane, one of Hope's old friends, approached me with a bright smile on her face.

I'm shocked. The last time I saw her was the day Charcoal came and took both of us away. She was taken as well. Although I knew the Crimson Powers weren't bad now, I was still surprised that they took Jane under their wing. "Wha- How?" I spit out, flabbergasted.

Jane just smiles and brings me into a hug. "It's been so long since I've seen you. I heard about your rescue by the Warriors." At the word rescue, Jane makes hand quotes, and rolls her eyes. "How are you?" She smiles again, and we embrace in a hug.

"I've been doing well. Wait, did they give you powers?" I say, wondering if they gave powers to everyone.

"No, not, yet. I must gain their trust first." She says, sounding envious. But I focus back as the other person tells me to lie down on the operating table. I immediately do, and out of the corner of my eye I can see the kid who's powers I am going to take lie down as well.

She looks scared, and she is hugging a stuffed bear tightly. I am about to comfort her when the lights turn on. I can feel a vibrating feeling throughout my body, but suddenly something changes. My heart beats out of my chest. I scream in pain, but it sounds like I'm underwater, and my voice is muffled. As I try to hold on, something pulls me back, and everything slowly fades to black.

I woke up in a white room. The walls are all white, and the door is sealed shut. I instinctively sit up, looking at my surroundings. "Where am I?" I mutter to myself. However, a voice answers. "Nye, we're keeping you here to help you learn your powers. This room will help you with your teleporting ability. It'll make sure that you can only teleport in this room."

For the fifth or sixth time in the day, I am startled. "How is that possible?" I inquired. I never heard of people being able to limit powers, much less teleportation. This time, Casper replied, saying that it was a recent discovery. The Crimson Powers managed to find specific items and materials that prevented certain powers. For example, Cypher was afraid of water, so Jonas could directly counter Cypher's power. By using teleportation, I would be able to leave a huge scar on the Liberti Warriors by revealing their bases and as a spy. However, I wasn't really sure that I wanted to help them do that.

I snapped back to reality, hearing Panther repeat my name. "Nye. Nye. Focus, kid. Try to teleport to the other side of the room." Panther shouted over the intercom. I nodded to show I was listening, and tried to focus, but I just couldn't do it. After trying my hardest, I sighed in defeat.

"How do I do it?" I complained, "Do I just imagine myself there or something?" This time, Casper spoke through the intercom.

"There is no trick. These powers are all personalized, so you have to find your way of doing it. The first time is always the hardest, Nye. You can do it," These words encouraged me, and I tried once again. This time I calmed myself down, thought of teleporting there, and suddenly I disappeared.

I felt myself stuck, in between reality and my imagination. I was in a blank space, drifting around. I couldn't move. I couldn't speak. My mind was hazy, until I remembered what I was supposed to do: teleport. In the next second, I was back in the room, but I moved. I was on the other side. I did it.

Casper and Panther were shouting and praising me for teleporting, but I just didn't care. Something felt...off. I didn't know where I was, who I was for a minute when I was in the in-between. What if these powers did something to me? What if these powers could hurt me? I tried to shrug the thought away, but it was like an itch at the back of my mind. It was like the power made sure that I never forgot. Like the power wasn't me, but another person entirely, and that person was tormenting me.

Chapter. 8

"Come on, Nye, you did this yesterday! Try harder, man!" Shouts from Panther do not help with my focus. It's been a few days since I first gained teleportation, and from the day that I managed to use it, Panther has been pushing me to new and higher limits. First, he asked me to teleport between rooms and floors, and now he's telling me to teleport between buildings.

The stress starts to build and I keep on losing focus more often. Finally, I snap. "Just be quiet! Let me concentrate!" The speaker projecting Panther's voice shuts up for a second, then Panther replies with a quick "fine" before the speaker shuts off again, this time for good.

I focus again on my surroundings, on where I want to go. In a quick second, I open my eyes to see myself successful. I try once again, focusing on a farther target and I do it once again. Finally, I set my sights on a building outside, around two miles away. I imagine myself and the surroundings there, and in a blink of an eye I'm at the building....or not. I open my eyes and feel it sting as

I am falling face first down the building. Looking around, I realize I may have teleported a little too far, but I quickly forget about that as I try frantically to not die.

I can feel my heart pounding in my chest as I continue to fall, each second closer to dying of falling. I slowly lose hope as I get closer and closer until I remember my power. I look up at the building's roof and imagine its surroundings. Just as I am about to faceplant on the floor, it goes dark.

I open my eyes and find myself at the crossroads once again. In nowhere. Slowly, I get to my feet and look around. For some reason, it looks familiar, but I can't put my grasp on it. Suddenly, I hear a faint whisper, and I swing around, only to see my reflection on a tinted yet darkened pool.

"Where am I?" I wonder aloud. Instead, I see something that scares the living daylight out of me. As if in a horror movie, my reflection begins to change, a wide sinister smile plastered on its face.

"You thought stealing powers wouldn't come with a cost?" The reflection grins and starts to move until he moves out of the mirror frame. I shake my head and imagine myself hallucinating. However, when I open my eyes, he's standing there, his smile even wider. He rushes at me, his eyes with a killer look.

Just as I begin to scream, I awake atop the building that I

planned on teleporting to. No one is in sight but I can see the faint outline of Panther staring at me from the window of the other building. His face has a displeased look. That's when I realized that I just left the building that guaranteed my safety.

I teleported back as fast as I could, but it was too late. Looking down from the window, I could see multiple people staring back at me, their mouths wide open. I was careless, and I let them learn about my power, which was supposed to be kept a secret.

At that moment, Panther burst into the room along with Casper and someone I didn't recognize. In a matter of minutes, they started to scold and berate me for the troubles I caused.

"What is wrong with you, Nye? Now that the civilians know about your power, word could spread to the Liberti Warriors. If you weren't so valuable, I would've kicked you out in a heartbeat." Panther shouts at me, cursing left and right. Looking at Casper, he has the same disappointed look as Panther, but he doesn't say anything.

We stand there for a moment in silence, before Casper breaks the silence: "Nye, I really wish that it wouldn't have come down to this, but you have forced our hand. This man is Devin, and he will be making sure that you stay. From now on, no wandering around this building. You will stay in your room and Devin will make sure of that. Copy?" Upon hearing this, I am shocked. How did they expect to keep me here with my powers?

"What did you say?" I reply, both angry and confused. "I'd like to see you try." I imagine myself once again in the other building, but nothing happens. I try harder, but it feels as if the power is all gone. "What did you do?" I exclaim in horror, worried that my powers are gone.

Instead, Devin responds. "My power is to disable powers around me. With me watching you, you won't be able to teleport." I'm shell shocked at the response, as I have never heard of someone whose power was to disable others. If they had Devin's power, it would give them an overwhelming advantage over the Warriors.

"Are you kidding me?" I yell, as if realizing for the first time that I was kidnapped. All my previous thoughts about the Crimson Powers emerged at once: how they were evil, how they kidnapped people, and more. I tried to teleport again, but still nothing happened. I glared at Devin, who leered at me.

"You brought this on yourself," Casper says. Devin and Panther take me by the arms and drag me once again into the room where I first learned teleportation. "You'll stay here until we know that you're trustworthy," Casper says, before shutting the door. I look around, only to see Devin sitting down in front of me.

"Just let me out, Devin, I didn't do anything," I try to reason, but Devin doesn't react as if he hasn't heard me.

I tried many more times that day, but I gave up after a while. I sat down and tried to get through the many more days left in the prison.

Chapter. 9

Hope

I wake up to the distant sound of punching and grunting. Slowly, I start to stir and look around, remembering where I was. For some reason, these past few days felt like a blur, as if I was living in a dream.

It takes a while before my eyes adjust to the surroundings, before I see someone standing in front of me. Charcoal is staring at me, his face devoid of emotion. "You're up," he states, and walks away.

At first, I am shocked at how rude he seems, but then I wonder if it was all just a front. Why was he standing in front of my bed in the first place? I wonder as I hastily get up, realizing I missed training for who knows how long.

I sprint towards the sounds of fighting, but as I turn the

corner it's not Echo or Void, but two people I don't recognize. One is pretty banged up, his face bruised and bleeding. He has blond hair, and at closer inspection electric tendrils zap around his body. The other person is much taller with dark hair and a huge tattoo on his face. He seems to have zero injuries, and he laughs at his opponent.

Charcoal notices me watching and beckons me over. "Hope, this is some of the Liberti Warriors, Cypher and Anesthesia. Anesthesia over here has passed my training recently, and he's here to spar with you."

At this, Anesthesia, the man with the face tattoo, stops boxing and looks at me with a glint in his eye. It takes me a while to catch on, but when I do, I don't believe it. "You want me to fight with a Warrior? I'm not strong enough, I'm just training." However, my comments don't seem to faze Charcoal.

"Don't worry, Hope, I'll go easy on you," Anesthesia chuckles at me. I ball my fists, making sure I maintain my cool.

"Fine, let's go," I responded, not letting Anesthesia get into my head. Charcoal seems satisfied with my response and leads us into the main boxing ring in the middle of the training room. There, I see Echo and Void on the sidelines. I wave to them, but for some reason Echo stares at me with a look in her eyes, like she's resentful of me.

We both approach the ring, getting ready. I suddenly remembered what happened before my blackout. My newfound power. This gives me lots more confidence, but then I realize that I don't know how I accessed that power.

Charcoal's voice brings me back to reality, and I stare at Anesthesia across me, who suddenly has a purple aura surrounding him. "Start!"

I barely register the word before Anesthesia yells, charging at me. I dodge out of the way, but not before taking a punch to my gut. All I can do is try to fight back with Charcoal's training, but it barely does anything.

I rush at Anesthesia, punching him multiple times in his stomach, but he just smiles and punches me across the face. I fall to the floor, dizzy and unaware that Anesthesia is charging once more.

I turn face up to see Anesthesia getting closer and closer. Suddenly, his fist comes closer to my face, before it disappears. I can see the look of confusion on Anesthesia's face as well, but I don't understand. At this moment, the purple aura around him fades, as he stares in disbelief. Then, I remember. My power. I look down, and as expected my whole body is made of water. At the corner of my eye, I can see Cypher's eyes light up in surprise, and Echo with her mouth open.

This time, I smile at Anesthesia before swinging my fist at him. Right when I connect, my fist turns solid. It doesn't do much to him, but I can see his surprise. I do it over and over again, as Anesthesia continues to stumble back. His punches do nothing to me. With every punch, I gain more confidence.

Suddenly, Charcoal's shout echoes once again. I turn back into human form and meet Charcoal's gaze. Charcoal looks different. For one, he doesn't look like he's about to kill someone. Instead, he's smiling.

"Nice job, Hope," he praises, before saying something to Anesthesia that I didn't hear. Cypher walks up to me and pats my back, laughing.

"That was interesting, Hope. I only know of a few people who have two powers." I blush at the amount of praise I'm receiving, but then I see Echo.

I rush over to Echo and Void, but Echo turns her back on me. "What's wrong?" I ask her, but she doesn't say anything. I look at Void, but of course she doesn't respond.

I ask again, and finally Echo turns around, but she's enraged: "What do you think? You suddenly appear and exceed all of Charcoal's expectations in the first few weeks you get here. I've been here for almost a year, how do you think you would feel if you were me?" Tears start to sprout out of her eyes, and she stomps off, followed by Void.

My heart breaks as I lose some of the only friends I gained these weeks. The other Liberti Warriors continue to praise me, and Anesthesia asks for a rematch, but all I can think about is what Echo told me.

Chapter. 10

The next few days were a blur. I was put through a few more trials, which I thankfully passed. After that, I was made an official Liberti Warrior, and not just in training. With my new advancement in the Warriors, there were many more duties I had to fulfill, which was almost enough to make me forget about my broken friendship. Almost.

These duties included late night patrols of the official Warrior base, scouting missions, and sometimes serving as backup in gang fights. However, one thing was still nagging on the back of my mind: where was my brother?

Lately, Charcoal has put me on more missions with different Warriors as a way for me to "get used to them". I've been put on missions with Cypher, Lightwave, and Anesthesia, sometimes even Charcoal. Every mission they surprise and impress me with their abilities, and I realize how much I got to catch up.

Finally, after a long day of patrol, I headed back into the main facility, looking forward to sleeping. Suddenly, I heard a rustle of bushes to my right. I immediately turn to the sounds, but all I see is a small rabbit, chewing on some grass. I breathe a sigh of relief and walk back to the compound when suddenly the sounds of chewing grass stop.

I spin to the direction of the sound and find myself face to face with a lady wearing fur pellets. Her hair is cut short and she is at least two heads taller than me. The lady bares her teeth at me before turning into a panther whose fur matches the color of the night. The panther lady lunges at me, but not before I turn my body into water.

The lady goes straight through me, and even with her animal form, I can tell she's surprised. However, it takes her less than a second to charge at me again, this time turning into a cheetah. I barely turn in time, and try to signal the Warriors for help. I rush over to sound the alarm, but she sees me, and pulls me back.

I punch her in the face and I hear her shout in agony, but I don't look back, instead rushing over to sound the alarm. The alarm bells ring throughout the compound, and in an instant Cypher appears, followed closely by Stinger and Lightwave.

The moment they appear, the lady begins to flee, but Stinger stops her. Since the panther lady could turn into animals, part of Stinger's power(to talk to and command animals) will also affect the lady. Stinger wills the lady to return and she does, her eyes turning milky white.

"Who's that?" Cypher asks me once the lady was locked in one of the interrogation rooms. I just shrug, and Cypher nods. "Get some sleep, then. We'll find out tomorrow with the help of Verity." For a moment there, I want to ask who Verity is, but I figured it's probably one of the other Warriors I hadn't met. I nod, then walk to bed, too tired to do anything else.

The next morning, I wake up to the sound of beeping and alarms: the alarms that signal a superpowered trespasser. I rush out the door after changing and observe three odd-looking figures that I don't recognize. I immediately rushed downstairs, only to find myself stopped by Anesthesia.

"Come with me, Hope," he said as Warriors started streaming out of their quarters, "Airless and the others can handle themselves."

"Are you sure?" I asked, but Charcoal started walking off, motioning for me to follow.

We reached one of the interrogation rooms when I finally realized what we were doing here: interrogating the shapeshift lady. Anesthesia slammed the door open, and I followed him in. Sitting in the middle of the room was the lady, although she looked a lot worse with bruises and blood dripping from her wounds. Was this type of torture really necessary?

Anesthesia got straight to the point: "Who are you and what do you want with us?" He asserted, but the lady doesn't respond. Instead, she let out a cackle that chilled me to the bone. For some reason, though, Anesthesia smiled. I was wondering why he was smiling, when I remembered something, or someone. Verity. The door opens, and who I assume is Verity walks in. As soon as she walks in, there is a sort of aura that surrounds the room. Verity strides over to the lady, although her hair is what distracts me the most. It's fully dyed red, with streaks of white.

Verity bends down and whispers into the lady's ear. Immediately, the lady starts to flinch, and she shivers, as if she is trying desperately to keep her secret. However, after just a few seconds, the lady spills everything.

"My name is Natalia Rose, and I work for the Crimson Powers. I was sent here to take out as many Warriors as I could to get ready for the coming invasion. The Crimson Powers have been distributing powers for loyal people to create an unstoppable army to take over the remaining world. We're here to destroy the last remaining thing that can ruin our plans." As soon as the lady, or Natalia, says that, she covers her mouth in a gasp. I stare in awe at Verity, imagining myself having truth powers. Verity smiles, but not before I remember what Natalia said.

"They're going to destroy the Liberti Warriors, how?" I ask, starting to worry. Verity repeats my question, and Natalia answers once again.

"A significant amount of the army is invisible right now, led by Jonas." The lady smiles once more. "They're here already." As soon as she finishes her sentence, a loud explosion rings outside.

I follow Anesthesia outside as we see a gaping crater where Cypher and the other Warriors we saw were standing. Waves of Crimson Power members equipped with superhuman abilities swarm the building. The Liberti Warriors were screwed. We looked on as the Warriors fell to the floor, either dying or getting subdued. I looked to Anesthesia, then at Verity. We were in for the fight of our lives.

Chapter. 11

I hear a wet thunk sound, and I turn to see someone sticking a dagger into Verity. Anesthesia. Her mouth opens, and I leap into action. Slamming my fist into Anesthesia's face, I hear a sickening crunch as he stumbles back, clutching his nose.

"Verity! Get up!" I yell, just as explosions sound in the distance. Verity manages a weak grumble before going limp. Luckily, her heart is still beating, so I took that to mean she fainted. In the blink of an eye, someone tackles me to the floor from my behind. Anesthesia. He lands one punch to my face before I turn to water, but that punch leaves me feeling concussed. I turn solid again and smack Anesthesia right in the face. He falls again, but the purple aura starts to appear around him, and I know it's only a matter of time before he turns invincible, so I do the only thing I can do; I grab Verity and run.

We run past explosions, rubble, and fallen warriors. All I can do is keep running as the building that once held the greatest heroes fell. Verity mumbles and I can feel her coming to her senses, but there's no time. A sudden blast of fire knocks me sideways, but it doesn't affect me much once I turn into water. Glaring at the person who shot at me, I quickly gain speed and fling myself at him, suffocating him with water. Once I know he's out cold, I pick up Verity again and keep running.

Just as I feel like I can't run anymore, a hand is placed on my back. With my reflexes, I hurriedly turn around and blast a ball of water at the person's face, but it turns out it was just Lightwave.

"Sorry, I thought you were one of the gangsters," I reply meekly, but she doesn't notice. Instead, she helps me pick up Verity and motions for me to follow her.

"I know a place we can hide. The Crimson Powers have taken many of the Warriors hostage, including Cypher, Charcoal, and Airless. I've managed to gather a few at this old, abandoned room connecting to the sewers, and I know you were with Anesthesia. Where is he?" Lightwave sounds so concerned that it makes me not want to tell her the truth, but I do anyway.

"Anesthesia betrayed us," I whisper, as Lightwave's face scrunches up in pain, "he was the one that knocked Verity out and told the Crimson Powers the location of our base. That's how they got my brother."

"No," Lightwave shakes her head, still not convinced, but at that moment Verity comes to. Somehow, she seems to have heard what we were saying, as she comes to my aid.

"It's true, Lightwave. Anesthesia's evil. I should've guessed, I could tell he was lying about something, I just didn't know it was important." Verity holds her head, and I hold her for support. Just then, Lightwave stops at a door concealed under the staircase.

She enters some kind of code, and the door swings open, revealing a few more people roaming around, some talking and others clearly agitated. I recognize a few of them, like Stinger and my old friends, Echo and Void. However, there are a few faces I don't recognize: two twins who are getting riled up.

As soon as Stinger sees Lightwave, her face lights up, and they start talking. I can tell when Lightwave brings up Anesthesia's betrayal based on Stinger's reaction. Her face first recoils in shock, then her eyes narrowed to slits. Lightwave then opens the door again, looking for more Warriors. Meanwhile, I turned to Verity, who sat down on the floor, her back resting against the wall.

"You okay?" I ask, but Verity just shushes me, needing rest. Not knowing what to do, I plop down next to Verity and sit there for a while, gathering my senses.

Suddenly, the door bursts open, and Lightwave marches in, dragging a man into the room. I immediately recognize him as the guy who blasted fire at me. What is he doing here? Lightwave throws him to the floor and it's clear the man is badly injured with many cuts and bruises covering his body.

He barely gets to his feet before Lightwave kicks him back down and asks the two brothers to hold him up, making sure he doesn't escape. Next, Lightwave beckons for Verity: "Make him tell us what's going on, Verity."

Verity approaches the man. Although she looks drained, she still manages to concentrate, using her powers: "Who are you, and what are you guys doing here?"

The silence in the room scares me, and for a split second I worry that Verity's powers aren't working. However, another second passes before I hear the man struggling, his attempts to say nothing failing.

"I'm Leo, I'm part of the Crimson Powers. We're here to take down the Liberti Warriors and collect the Warrior's special powers to give to our people." The answer leaves us stunned. They were trying to drain our powers, and they already got Cypher, Charcoal, and Airless.

"Where did your friends take the captured Warriors?" Verity asks, although she too seems disturbed by the information.

Leo can't hold anything from Verity, and he spills everything. "They took the prisoners to the main base, which is about a five day walk from here. The main base is under a street still run by Dreads."

Lightwave straightens up at the mention of the Dreads. "Didn't Airless kill them all?" Leo just laughs, and shakes his head.

"There are so many more Dreads that Airless didn't uncover. When Airless was massacring the Dreads, the ones still in hiding ran for Mexico. Over the past few years, they have gained exponentially in numbers and strength, all because Airless gave them a reason. They didn't even kill Nova!" Leo keeps on laughing, but everyone picks up on the last sentence.

"Who killed Nova?" Verity says, uncertainty in her voice.

Leo looks around the room, his eyes landing on each of us. The corners of his mouth twitch, his face plastered with an eerie grin. "He's not dead," he cackles, "we have him."

Chapter. 12

"He's still alive, and we know where they're holding him! Shouldn't we go and save him and the rest of the captured Warriors?" Stinger exclaims, though you can hear the anxiousness in her voice.

"Stinger, we all want to save Nova and the others, but we don't have a plan. We're in a bad position. Almost all of the Warriors are gone, and we're all split up. Meanwhile, the Crimson Powers have actual powers and have some of our strongest fighters captured. All that's left of us are two kids who haven't even passed training, two siblings that barely passed, and you, me, Verity, and Hope!" These words stream out of Lightwave, until she is shouting at us.

"Guys, I think we should just calm down, and think about what we can do next," I say, trying to stop the two from arguing. Luckily, it seems to work. Lightwave takes a deep breath, and mumbles a "sorry" at Stinger.

From the other side of the room, someone raises their hand.

One of the twins. "I got an idea, why don't we just use Leo to get in?" Although it is an interesting idea, it would never work, but I don't say it to his face. Instead, I ask for his name.

"I'm Multi, and my brother is Boost. He has super speed, while I can create replicas of myself." Stinger seems to know them, but I never met them before. However, Multi's powers intrigue me. Cloning?

Stinger rolls her eyes and stands up. "Enough with the introductions, we still need to think of a plan, and fast. We can't stay here forever."

"Stinger's right," Verity says, "there's no food in here, so we should try and leave this room. We can think of a plan later." Knowing Verity is right, everyone agrees to leave the room. Lightwave enters the door code, and Stinger and I go out first to scan the surroundings.

Seeing it's clear, we beckon for the others to follow. We scan around the building, but find no food or survivors. Instead, we pass multiple bodies of Warrior and gang members alike.

"It seems like the Crimson Powers left," Echo whispers to the group, but I'm still wary. Suddenly, a loud bang comes from the right, and as a group we instinctively turn. Creeping up the corner, we are all ready for an encounter with a hostile, but as we turn, we realize it's a dead body.

All of a sudden, a fireball blasts so close to my face that my heart skips a beat. Leo. Amidst the chaos, he must've escaped his binds. I turned around, ready to confront him but the others reacted. Boost becomes a blur, rushing around Leo and punching him. Finally, Lightwave shoots a blast of energy into Leo's chest, causing him to get pushed back and fly into the wall with a sickening crack.

"Thanks", I say, as we continue to search for food.

After a long time of searching, we still came up with nothing. "What are we supposed to do?" Echo complains, but Stinger shushes her.

"We have to find someplace else," I come to Echo's aid. "We've looked everywhere, maybe there's someplace outside the base that has food." The majority agree with me, other than Stinger, so we head on our way. Remembering that our goal is still to save our captured friends, we set off in old Mexico's direction.

Minutes turn to hours, and hours turn to days. Members in our group start to fall behind. Boost is the first to stop, his recent use of power draining all his energy. Sadly, he's not the only one. The ones in our group who can go on do, but each day's a new struggle.

Finally, as the last of us fall to hunger and thirst, we find a warehouse. At first, I thought I was dreaming. Stinger, Echo and

I dragged the other Warriors into the building. It felt unreal, with stacks and stacks of canned food and running water all around us.

Not having the strength to talk, the three of us shove bite after bite into our mouths, until we all feel stuffed to the brim. We then shake awake the others and let them eat.

"This is the best I've felt in a while," exclaims Verity as we all nod, agreeing. Suddenly, a shout echoes from the back of the warehouse. Instantly, I turn towards the sound, and the others do, too. My heart pounds as the seconds pass.

As three people turn around the corner, we are about to attack until Verity shouts "NO!". The three people turn and see Verity, but for some reason, they start to grin once they see us.

"Verity! We thought all the Warriors were captured!" One of them yells in glee, and he rushes forward, embracing Verity with a hug.

"How do you know them?" Stinger asks, a hint of suspicion in her voice.

"We were in training together," Verity replies, "Torch and Ingot passed before me, and Blizzard and I passed together." At this, I relax. If they escaped, maybe there's more out there.

"Well, I'm happy that you guys could reunite, but we still got people to save," Lightwave states. However, some of the others are still too tired, and Torch, Ingot, and Blizzard are confused.

"Lightwave, I think we should stay here, just for a little while. Most of our group are still tired, and we haven't informed Verity's friends about our plan." I try to reason with Lightwave. At my words, Lightwave seems to relax a little.

"Fine," she grumbles, "we can rest here. But only for a few hours," she adds before sinking to the floor.

As the others slowly start to fall asleep, I approach Torch, Ingot, and Blizzard. Ingot had already fallen asleep, but the others were still up, talking.

"Hey," I whisper, not wanting to wake up the others, "there's something I need to ask you guys. I was just wondering if you wanted to help us with our rescue plan?"

"What do you mean?" Torch replies, a suspicious look suddenly plastered on his face.

"The Crimson Powers captured many of our friends, and we managed to capture one of them. Using Verity's power, we were able to learn where their base was located, so we are planning to go there and rescue them from the gang. It would be nice if you three would join us. We need every person we can get." As soon as I finish, Torch's face turns somber.

"I can't speak for Ingot and Blizzard, but I'm not going. Why would you guys confront them again? If you don't remember, they took out all the Liberti Warriors. We're lucky to be alive!" I try to persuade him, but he doesn't budge. Reluctantly, I let Torch and Ingot walk away, leaving me with Blizzard.

Blizzard, unlike Torch, looks torn. "Please," I beg him. "We can't just let the Crimson Powers do whatever they want. They are planning to give away the powers of the captured Warriors, and with that they will become invincible." Blizzard stands there, his forehead wrinkled. Finally, he grins, and nods. Relief floods through my body and I can't help but smile: we're one step closer to saving the captured Warriors.

Chapter. 13

Nye

"Wake up! Casper wants to see you," a voice shouts through the intercom. Dazed and sleep deprived, I stumble towards the sound, only to see the door to my cell open.

"What the hell?" I mutter to myself as I walk out the door, my head throbbing. At the door entrance stands two guards, both with guns in their arms.

"Follow," they say in monotone, then march off down the corridor. Hurrying along, I skip a few steps and catch up to them before they turn left. And right. And left. And right. On and on they go, twisting and turning so many times until I'm lost.

After what seems like a millennia, the two guards stop in front of a huge, medieval-looking door swung open. What I saw next made my jaw drop. The room made the door look tiny, as hordes of people walked around. In the middle of the room housed a huge cage.

My eyes started to focus on the people inside the cage. To my surprise, it was Charcoal and a bunch of other Liberti Warriors. Then I saw him. Standing right next to Charcoal was none other than Airless himself, his yells echoing across the room. "How are none of the Warriors escaping?" I mumbled to myself, but someone replied: "These bars are not just any type of steel; they're made of a specific metal that cancels out powers, just like how Devin's power works." I whirl around to see Casper. When did he get here?

It took all my willpower to stop me from charging at Casper, who was one of the people who put me in the cell. However, I knew I had to behave, and Devin was still blocking my powers, so there was nothing I could do. Then, I remembered. My sister. Last I remembered, she was still with Charcoal.

Ignoring the warnings and shouts from Casper, I rush towards the cage, hoping that she's there and unharmed. "Hope! Hope!" I yell as I frantically look around the cage. I keep on shouting her name until a hand yanks my collar and pulls me near the cage. I freaked out for a second, worried that they thought I was the one who captured them, until I saw who it was: Charcoal.

"Listen, Nye. Your sister wasn't with us when we got captured, so there's a chance she's still alive. You got to help us get out of here, though, got it?" I don't even have a chance to nod before Charcoal starts talking again. "Turn off whatever is shutting our powers down, then we can fight our way out of here."

"Contain the prisoner!" Shouts Casper, and guards immediately start to approach.

"What happened?" Casper asks me as he gets closer to me, flanked by two guards on either side.

"Nothing," I say, "the Warrior just wanted to beat up the people who put him here." Casper looks at me for what feels like a long time before pointing to one of the guards walking around: "Make sure something like this doesn't happen to him again." The guard salutes Casper and replies with a "yes, sir" before turning his head to me.

"Thanks, I guess?" Casper laughs, probably at my reaction, and motions for me to follow him.

"Sorry you had to stay in the cell for such a long time, we just had to make sure you didn't do anything like that again. We didn't know if we could trust you since you had ties to the Warriors, and the stunt you pulled scared us for a minute." Casper looks at me with a pitied look in his eye, and I almost lose it, scrunching my hands into fists. Obviously, Casper notices that too and sighs.

"I can't blame you for not trusting us, Nye, but I was

hoping I could offer something as a negotiation, like maybe more responsibilities?" At this, my head jerks up. I could learn more about the Crimson Powers and I would be able to find out how to break the Warriors out of their cage!

"What do you mean?" I ask, slightly intrigued.

"I mean more assignments, less training. Since you've gotten a handle on your teleporting, you would be very helpful in many major missions. Also, you would have more command, more soldiers, and more free time." Even though I was planning on getting revenge, this offer did sound sweet, and when did the Warriors care about me when I had no powers? Maybe this was a better deal.

Then, I remembered something. If I saved them, they could help me find my sister. I knew I had to decide fast, on which side I was on, and I did. I would help the Warriors. But I wasn't one of them. Saving Hope would be my first priority, then we would run. Away from this. These troubles.

"Totally," I reply, faking a smile. Casper laughs and extends his hand and we shake. Then, he starts talking again.

"For now, I'll have someone you know to follow you around and give you the tour." He points to the elevator, which has just opened. In comes Jonas, a sly grin on his face as he saunters across the room, stopping to chat to people along the way.

Jonas. He seemed nice at the start, but now he just looks like an arrogant prick. However, I wave at him. He sees me and his grin turns to a smile.

"Nye, my guy!" He chuckles and slaps me on the back.

"Jonas, what have you been up to?" I ask him, noticing another scar etched on his face, marking a huge scar.

Jonas notices me staring, and laughs. "This?" He says, pointing at his scar, "this was nothing. It was worth it, capturing those scum." He then stares at the Warriors in the cage.

"How are you guys doing?" he shouts across the room, straight at the Warriors. Some turn to look at him, but the majority just turn to each other, whispering something that I can't make out.

"Are you guys comfortable in your cage?" he shouts again, and many other Crimson Powers start to catcall. Still, they don't respond, although I can make out a few who visibly seem disturbed by Jonas's taunting.

Jonas shrugs, and turns back to me and Casper. "I tried." He says nonchalantly, as Casper rolls his eyes. That's when I remember something else.

"Casper, isn't your brother in the cage as well? Aren't you going to talk to him?" As soon as these words left my mouth, I knew I said something wrong. Casper's face seems to swell up, and his hands bunch up into fists.

"I have given him a chance to reconcile. He's dead to me."

Chapter. 14

It takes a while for Casper to recompose himself, but when he does, he gives orders to Jonas, instructing him on what to do.

"Aye aye, sir," Jonas salutes sarcastically, leaving Casper to grumble. "Follow, Nye," Jonas says as he immediately strides off. As we walk, he talks to me about a few things left and right, which I don't really care about. However, as we finally near the door, something piques my interest.

"What's that?" I ask, pointing to a hidden corner. Engraved in tiny letters are a bunch of names. Half of them are very clearly carven, while others are fainter. There are a few names that are scratched off, and I can barely make them out.

"It's nothing," Jonas shakes off the question, but I can make out a tense tone in his voice. I remind myself to investigate further as Jonas opens the door and I follow him.

As soon as I walk in, there's a bright pillar of light. I squint, not used to the brightness, and it takes me a minute or so to realize that I'm in a room with bunk beds all around. "Where are we?" I ask, bewildered. A huge glass window is the roof, which explains the light.

"This is where you're going to live," Jonas mentions. "What? You think we were going to throw you back in your cell?" He grins, then approaches a bed. 'You're going to be bunking with Smithy, he's going to teach you what you need to know."

I want to ask him what he means, but he has already started moving to the next room. Hurriedly, I rush after him, turning around the corner and what I see next shocks me more than the previous room did. Jonas leads me to a huge dome-like room as bright as the living quarters. All around, sounds of grunts and punches echo. I recognize a few of them: Leo, who had the power of fire, and Jane, slamming her fists into a punching bag. Wait, what was that? Jane's fists, they turned to what seemed like concrete, then back to normal.

Not bothering to listen to Jonas, I rushed forward, closing in on Jane. "Jane!" I shout, and she turns her head, confused. When she sees me, she smiles, but I don't care.

"What did you just do?" I wheeze out, as Jane seems confused. Suddenly, I can see her face widen in realization.

"Right, I forgot you didn't know. Panther gave me powers! He said I was ready and now I can change by command." She seems happy, and I breathe a sigh of relief.

"I thought you were changed into one of their soldiers," I whisper to her, "it's good you got powers now, too. You can help me with rescuing the Warriors."

Jane frowns, her eyes turning to slits, "why would you want to help those villains escape?" Her voice is full of accusation and anger, and the empty feeling in my stomach rises again.

"Jane, whatever they told you, they're lying. I talked to Charcoal, and he told me about what they were doing. If we get them out, we can meet up with Hope and the other Warriors." I desperately try to talk sense into her, but she doesn't budge.

"Because we were old friends, and I understand what it's like to be brainwashed, I'm not going to tell anyone about this. But this is the last time. One more word and I'll tell Panther about you."

I shake my head in defeat, knowing there's nothing I can do. A childhood friend, gone like that. I walk back to Jonas, and try to act nonchalant, but Jonas sees straight through me.

"What were you talking about with that girl?" He says, suspicion creeping into his sentence.

"Nothing," I dismiss him, but he stares a bit longer at me before finally letting it go.

He leads me through the room, introducing me to some of the other people: Xavier, who spits acid, Betty, who can control people, Malik, who has super strength, and Donna, who can turn invisible. As we make our way back around, Jonas pulls me aside.

"Nye, look. You're a bright kid, but I know you're not trying to make friends. In here, it's a battle to the death. Without teammates, there's no way you can make it in here. Not all recruits are nice." Nice. Jonas is giving me a pep talk now.

"I know that, Jonas, but I can handle myself." Jonas stares at me again, before sighing and taking me to the next room.

The other rooms aren't as special as the first two, with kitchens and toilets. Finally, after what seems like forever, Jonas brings me back to the dorms. It had already turned to night outside, and there were other people in the dorms. Jane, Malik, and Betty were all here, as were many more. I plopped myself onto the bed, and immediately tried to sleep, but someone tapped me on the shoulder.

I opened my eyes to find Malik in front of my bed. "Oh hey, Malik." I said, but Malik laughed. He was much meaner than me now compared to before. Then again, Jonas was there. Now he wasn't.

"Newbie, you seem weak. What's your power?" He taunted, throwing my pillow to the floor.

I was done with all of this. After a long day, I was tired, and not being able to sleep made me mad. "Give me back my pillow, Malik," I warned, but he didn't seem to get it.

"What are you going to do if I don't? Punch me?" He laughed, then his eyes turned to slits. "I punch the hardest here, newb." I could predict it before he even moved. He was going to punch me. Lucky for me, I could teleport. Right before his fist connected, I teleported behind him.

He missed, and his fist hit the wall. I slammed his head into the bunk bed, the wood splintering. As he got up, the left side of his face was extremely red, but otherwise fine. "Stop it, Malik," I told him, "I just want to sleep. Next time you try to do something, I will do something much worse to you." His eyes went wide, and he backed off. Finally, I could sleep.

Chapter. 15

The next morning, I awoke to an overwhelming wave of sound. I rubbed my eyes and sat up, remembering that I was bunking with a group of complete strangers. For some reason, they were all up at the crack of dawn.

I saw Betty rush past me and managed to keep her from running off. "What's going on? It's like 6 in the morning," I exclaimed, but she seemed anxious.

"You're not ready yet? The leaders of the Crimson Powers are coming today because of our capturing of the Warriors. They're notorious for lashing out at any small thing!"

"Damn it," I grumbled, "why do I have such bad luck?" I tried to talk to Betty again but she already ran off. Not wanting to get on the bad side of the top gang bosses, I rushed out of bed and began getting my things sorted, but the door suddenly opened. In came Panther, followed closely by four men. This was the first time I'd seen Panther since I got locked up, but he looked no different. However, one of the four men, who I could only assume were the top leaders, looked painstakingly familiar. A tall man, he seems to be the youngest out of the four. Other than a bruised nose, he bore no battle scars.

The rest of the people stand at attention when they come in, and all I can do is follow, even though my bed was still a complete mess. My heart hammers in my chest as the leaders walk around the room. Finally, they stop at me.

"What's wrong with your bed? Do you not know how to clean up after yourself?" One of the leaders asks, and I bite my lip to stop me from talking back. They walk on, but not before giving me disapproving glances.

As soon as they leave, some of the people nearby start smirking, including Malik. "So sad," he chuckles, "aren't you worried you're going to get kicked out?" Up until then, I hadn't fully realized the consequences. Did they actually have the authority to kick someone out? Then again, they were the leaders, other than Casper.

"Shut up," I spat back at him, "worry about yourself." Malik's face turned red, but the previous night's confrontation was probably still fresh in his mind, because he cleared off.

The rest of the day sucked, and I was living in an apocalypse. Really puts it in perspective. Jonas forgot to mention the three hour training sessions right after breakfast, and just when the training finished, the testing began.

Apparently, the leaders were here to find the elite of the Crimson Powers to join them on a mission. What the mission was, no one knew, but the thought of moving up the ranks caused significant tension within the people in my room. For me, though, I didn't really care cause I was still working on helping the Warriors escape. Constant fights and bickering went on throughout the day, and if that wasn't enough, I was paired with Malik for duo training. With Malik unwilling to listen to me, we got destroyed by almost every pair, making us finish in the bottom half. Even the tests were bad. There were multiple questions on routine and what if scenarios, and since I had no previous training before, I couldn't answer any of them.

By the end of the day, I had accumulated a massive headache. I was so tired that as soon as the lights went out, I was knocked out cold.

My eyes open to gusts of wind coming from all around me. Where am I? I desperately try to look around, seeing if anything sparks my memory, to no avail. Suddenly, the winds stop, leaving me standing in darkness, with silence all around me.

"Hello?" I shout, but my voice just echoes, getting softer and softer. As my voice drifts away from me, a bright pillar of light appears, and in the middle stands the child with the teddy bear, whose powers I took. Only this time, her eyes are pearl white, and there is an unmistakable aura around him.

"You took my powers," the child starts to say, although her face still has that blank expression, "you took them from me." I am both confused and shocked as to where I am, and how she got here.

"What's going on?" I ask him, but as I start to approach, she disappears again, just to reappear behind me. A familiar feeling started to flow through me, like I wasn't myself. I could feel my powers slowly separate from my body, and I shuddered in response.

"What are you doing? Stop it!" I yell, but she doesn't acknowledge what I just said. Instead, she teleports again, this time closer, and pushes me to the floor.

"You took my powers," she repeats louder, and I try to get up, only to get pushed again. Although she looked like a child, she certainly had much more strength than one.

"You agreed to it," I shouted, bewildered at what was going on. However, the child just stares and points at her chest. I am stunned as blood spreads across her white shirt. What is happening?

I rush over to help her, but it seems like she isn't fazed by the blood. She pushes back at me and says one last thing before she faints: "You killed me."

I gasp as I wake up from that horrible dream. Although that was a dream, the child's final words still gave me shivers. Was it really true? What if the Crimson Powers killed those children? That made it more important to stop them, and save the Warriors. How would I do it, though?

Chapter. 16

My headache, which normally gets better after sleep, seemed to be growing worse. I gritted my teeth as wave after wave of nausea hit me, leaving me barely able to stand. Jane, who I haven't talked to in days, seems to notice my condition and comes to help, but I push her off with a shrug.

My vision starts getting blurry, and it feels like I'm about to vomit. Just then, the gang leaders walk in. Damn it, I thought to myself. Could I make my reputation any worse? As they approach, I try to control the increasing pain in my head, and I manage to hold out for a few more minutes. However, as they approach my bunk bed, I just can't take it any longer, and scream out in pain. Clutching my head and my eyes scrunched shut, I stumbled around blindly and hit the floor.

I hear mutters and gasps around me, but I couldn't care less about them. All I cared about now was stopping the pain in my head. Then, it's gone. For a second, I'm stunned. Then, I realize the pain has stopped, and I'm relieved. Standing up, it felt awkward to have everyone staring at me.

"I'm fine," I say, a bit embarrassed, "my head just started to hurt a bit." However, I notice something isn't right. Why were they all staring at me like that? Even the gang leaders had their eyes popping out of their face, like they had just seen a miracle. I looked down, and saw my whole body on fire. "What the fu-?" I muttered as my legs gave in and I fell to the floor, unconscious.

I woke up to bright lights shining in my face, and a jumble of voices from all around me. Groggily, I lift myself up and rub my eyes, but when my eyes start to focus, I realize I'm on the floor, with almost everyone huddled around me.

"What was that?"

"How'd you do that?"

"I thought you could teleport."

"Two powers?"

Word after word, question after question, voice after voice. They swarm at me until I can't take it anymore. "Stop!" I yell in frustration, but I'm surprised once again when I realize that my hands are clutching fire. Then I remember. Fire surrounding my body, then blacking out. What just happened to me?

One voice grabs my attention: Panther. "How? I've never heard of someone who had two powers." I look towards his voice, and realize he's not talking to me. Instead, he's muttering to the

Crimson Leader with the bruised nose.

"I don't know, but it's got to be related to his sister." At this, my ears perk up. How did this guy know Hope? "She got a second power as well, just a few weeks ago." Hope? Could it be? Getting up, I wave the others away, but the leaders stay.

One of the leaders, easily the oldest of the four, takes one step closer. "How'd you get that power?" He asks, but I shrug, genuinely having no clue of what I just did. The leader looks a bit disappointed, but it disappears in a flash. "Never mind that. You would make a valuable member on our strike team," he smiles, and extends his hand. "The name's Scythe." I put on a smile, but I can't ignore the leader with the bruised nose.

"How did you know my sister?" I ask, and the leader just scoffs.

"You don't recognize me? I saw you in the Warriors headquarters." And I remember. Anesthesia. The one with invulnerability. Before I can say another word, he speaks again: "You see this bruise? That was your sister's fault." He spits on the floor, a scowl on his face.

Just then, Panther cuts in, pushing Anesthesia back. Although he seems pissed, Anesthesia stands down. Panther approaches me, an apologetic look plastered on his face, but I know better. Panther is acting just as much as I am. "Sorry about him, he's just mad. Everyone, leave!" He shouts, and almost everyone leaves, leaving me and the leaders, along with Panther. "Let's talk about the mission." At this, I can't help but smile. I'm one step closer to rescuing Airless and the others.

Scythe and Anesthesia lead me and a few others around the compound. Left. Right. Down a flight of stairs. Finally, we reach another darkened room, hidden from sight. Opening the door, I walk in and find a room that kind of looks like a meeting area, with a huge round table and maps on all four sides. "Sit," Scythe motioned to us. I took a seat next to Anesthesia and someone else I didn't recognize.

Looking around, I noticed both Jane and Malik among the chosen ones for this mission. Malik. I can't help but grimace, but I remind myself of the mission. I have to save the Warriors. Scythe opens his mouth: "Each of you have been chosen for a specific role in this mission. As you probably heard, this is probably one of the hardest ones we've had so far. We will be hunting down some of the remaining Warriors, including some of the most powerful ones. Lightwave, Verity, Stinger, and most recently, a Warrior that has gained two powers: Hope." Her name sends a jolt through me. They're hunting my sister. I try to ignore the dread in my body, but words burst out.

"What are you going to do with them?" I shout, inadvertently standing up.

Once again, Panther comes to intervene. "We're not going to harm your sister. Once the others are obtained, we can make sure that she's not brainwashed by the Warriors." Although those words were supposed to calm me, they didn't. However, I still had to keep it together. I mumble a sorry and sit down, allowing Scythe to continue.

"As I was saying, each of you have your own responsibilities. Copycat," he then points at a large and buff dude with tattoos across his face, "you will use your copying abilities to mimic Stinger and hopefully incapacitate her. Malik and Jane, you will fend off the other Warriors who escaped. And Nye, you will go head-to-head against your sister." What? It felt like I was in the arena, pitted between surviving and killing my best friend. "We are not trying to pit you against each other. You're the only person we have right now that has two different powers, especially teleportation. You could be the way that we get in and out of tough situations. It's only fitting that you take on your sister, who might be one of the strongest Warriors left."

Just then, the doors to the compound burst open. A tall lady bursts in, blood dripping down her face. "RUN!" she shouts just as the alarms to the compound start ringing.

Chapter. 17

We leave Torch and Ingot the very next day. They provided us with a few days' worth of food, but both refused to come with us, scared of putting their lives in danger. We headed off immediately, with only an objective in mind: go to Mexico and save the captured Warriors.

"Can't I just run there with super speed and bust them all out?" Boost whines as we continue to walk. I sigh and begin to speak, but Echo intervenes.

"How many times do we have to tell you? The Crimson Powers now have supers, and their base will be extremely fortified. There's no point. Anyways, you don't have enough energy to bring us all there." Boost sighs and stands down for now, but I can tell that the group is starting to get anxious. Trudging along the sides of old roads, we stumble across another one of the smaller, gang-run cities. Just like my old home. However, one thing stops me in my tracks. The symbol on the conquest flags across this village. It was similar, but at the same time, I didn't recognize it. I'm about to ask the others, but they stopped, too. It wasn't only me. Echo's eyes widened, and that's when I remembered. Her tattoo, the same exact logo around the city.

"Guys, stop," I yelled at the rest of the group.

Lightwave is the first to turn around, annoyed: "We can't just be stopping at random places. We've got to find the others!" However, as I point at Echo's tattoo, and she makes the connection for herself, her eyes widen. "Echo, who are they? And why have you gotten their logo tattooed on your freaking arm?"

Echo sighed, shaking her head, but her eyes still lingered on the flags. "Nothing. It's fine, nothing to see here, let's keep going."

Echo spoke a little too fast for it to sound genuine, and apparently, Verity thought so too. "Echo, tell us the truth. I don't want to have to use my power on you." Looking at Echo's face, it seemed like she just realized that, too, and immediately her face went pale.

"Fine, fine. They were the gang that ruled my home. Money Makers, or that's what they called themselves." I looked at Verity to confirm Echo wasn't lying, and she nodded.

"Then why do you have that tattoo?" I continue to press, but Echo just glares at me.

"None of your business," she snaps at me, and starts to walk away. Just as I'm about to push further, shouts from the distance startle me. I turn back towards the village as a group of people emerge and shout at us to stop.

"Look, it's all a misunderstanding," Lightwave begins to talk with the group, but they don't listen. Instead, one of them points at Echo, and they stare in disbelief. Apparently, Echo hasn't told us the whole story. Just when Lightwave begins to say something else, one of the people grab Echo. Instinctively, Blizzard shoots a freeze ray at the person and Echo escapes their grasp. However, this action brings the whole group to a frenzy. In less than a second, chaos emerges.

All I can see is a man burst into flame before someone else charges at me. The man's hand shoots out zaps of electricity, nearly striking me in the chest. I dodge out of the way at the last second, hearing the zap in the air. Too close. Changing into my water form, I prepare to move through the man when I get striked by a lightning bolt. Immediately, a thousand jolts rip through my body, and I fall to my knees. Through my blurred vision, I can see that I turned back to human form. Of course, electricity and water.

Writhing in pain, I manage to make out the man over me, about to blast me again. At that moment, I knew that I had to get up, but even if I did, I couldn't do anything against him. Turning into a body of water would make me even more vulnerable, and breathing underwater is entirely useless here. I desperately push myself up, but it's already too late. Tendrils of electricity are aimed straight at my face, zapping the air around me.

"Thank you for bringing back Ella, but we'll take it from here," he snarls. If I wasn't in a life-or-death situation, I would've asked about that, but there was no time. And who the hell was Ella? The last thing I saw was the electricity getting closer and closer, wishing I could do something about it.

Then, everything went black.

I opened my eyes. I was still alive. But something was different. Something felt different. Looking down, my body was not in human form. But also not in water form. Instead, it was on fire, flames burning where my body was supposed to be. "What... How...?" I was at a loss for words, and so was the man with the electricity powers. The man who attacked me. I come back to my senses and drive my fiery hand through his chest, burning him. Then, I turn solid and knock him out with a punch.

Looking around, I notice that almost everyone has finished their fight. The remaining people who weren't on the floor, assumedly the Money Makers, ran back the way they came.

"Finally," Stinger grumbles as she turns from a tiger back to a human. "That was a good warm-up, but let's keep moving." Just as these words leave her mouth, more shouts come from the distance. The Money Makers that left came back with reinforcements. A lot of them. In the front stood a tall, burly man with the Money Makers logo tattooed on his face. He was definitely the leader, as everyone else seemed like they were staring at him for further instructions.

"Dang it," Blizzard, who I didn't even realize was behind me, spoke. I was ready to fight, especially with my newfound fire ability.

Just then, the leader spoke up. "Everyone, stand down! We didn't mean to hurt you, it's just that you guys have Ella. We thought you guys were the ones who kidnapped her."

Lightwave spoke for all of us: "Who's Ella? We've never heard of her," but the leader just points at Echo. Echo's real name was Ella?

We were still confused, and I cut in: "What do you mean, kidnap her? And why should you care?" Echo looked down at the floor, looking guilty.

The leader opened his mouth and said something that left me shocked: "I am Eli, and Ella's my daughter."

Chapter. 18

"What?" How did I never hear of this? I looked to Echo, hoping that she wasn't actually the daughter of a gang leader. Nevertheless, the look of guilt on her face told me who was lying.

"We were a great team," Eli continued, "we would track down people that went against us, and she would…convince them to stop giving us any trouble." He passed at the word convinced, inferring Echo, or Ella's use of her powers. "And then out of nowhere, she left. Not a word. No warning at all. I assumed she had been kidnapped, and we searched a few of the villages around us. I can't believe that we found you, Ella." Although I understood Eli, I couldn't bring myself to tell him that his daughter chose to join the Warriors. She wasn't kidnapped, she had run away.

As Eli approached Ella, he wrapped his arms around her, hugging her tightly. However, Ella didn't do the same. Instead, her arms lay stiff around her sides. Apparently, Eli didn't notice, but I did. Before I could say anything, though, Eli smiled, and motioned for us to follow him. Not wanting to anger him and the huge group of people behind him, we followed him further into the village. Everywhere we looked, the village people cowered in their houses, or stayed far away. What did Eli's gang do to them?

I wanted to talk to Echo to clear up some of the questions I had, but she was already dragged away by her father, and surrounded by his henchmen. "What are we going to do?" I mumbled to Lightwave, and she shrugged.

We walked into some sort of building that looked like a town hall, although there were many banners of the Money Makers everywhere. "This is our base here," Eli shouted over the other noises. "We will provide you guys with some food and water for the misunderstanding that was caused. Then, you guys can go on your merry way."

I was surprised that Eli was that nice, as almost all my previous encounters with gangs were not as smooth. All of us muttered thanks, but we weren't really as hungry because of all the food from the warehouse. However, we didn't want to seem ungrateful of Eli's kindness, so we reluctantly accepted. Boost, for one, was happy for all that food, and ate like a madman, engulfing plate after plate of food.

Finally, with our ever-fuller stomachs, it was time for us to leave. Eli and a few more of his guards brought us out and handed us a few more bags of food. "Thank you for taking care of Echo, and I wish you well on your trip."

Just as I was about to thank him, Blizzard intervened. "Wait, where's Echo?" Looking around, I realized Blizzard was right. Throughout our time in the town hall, Echo had vanished. Eli grimaced, and in a flash, I knew what happened.

"Where'd you take Echo?" I yelled, not able to hide my anger, "we never agreed to leave her behind. She's a Warrior!" This time, Eli's seemingly calm facade broke, leaving him seething.

"She's my daughter! I will not allow her to leave again!" The guards to the left and right of him both step forward, as if synchronized, putting themselves between Eli and us. "You know," Eli continues, "I really hoped that it wouldn't have come to this, but you leave me no choice. Execute them." With that simple command, Eli walks off, leaving the handful of guards to deal with us.

"We just beat a group of your gang members that was twice this group's size!" Stinger yells mockingly at Eli, but then I notice something. They're not the only ones. From the village, what seems like a hundred people run at us, eyes shining with malice. "I take it back", Stinger mutters as they all run at us. I get ready for battle, although it seems impossible for us to win this fight.

Just then, I hear a shout from afar. I can't make out anything, but it sounds suspiciously familiar. Then, Echo appears, running out of the town hall with Eli in fast pursuit. "Stop!" She shouts just as we collide with the gang members. And surprisingly, they all stop. Every single one of them. Bewildered, I look to Echo and see her with the same shocked expression that I had.

"Echo, your powers!" I shout in glee, momentarily forgetting that we were still caught in an angry gang leader's path. Echo smiles, but suddenly gets pulled back by her father. Eli's eyes are crazed, and they dart around, staring at each one of us.

"Go away," he yells, "Echo's staying with me." Knowing that in this state, Eli is already beyond reason, I ask Void to make Eli calmer. Void nods, and after a few seconds her power's effects start to show. Eli's eyes stop darting around, and he lets go of Echo. In fact, he starts walking away.

"What did you do to him?" I ask, bewildered, and Void just shrugs. There's no time for me to ponder that question, as Echo rushes to us, a smile on her face.

"Void! You can control your powers!" She shouts in glee, and the two embrace in a hug. However, it's quickly broken up by Lightwave, who reminds us of our mission. So, we pack up and get our stuff ready, with a better control of our powers and an abundant amount of food. But one question still nagged me at the back of my mind: Did I unlock all my powers yet? And if I didn't, how would I?

Chapter. 19

After days and days of walking, we finally reach the streets owned by the Dreads. Just from entering the city that once used to be Mexico, we could tell it was taken over. Just like the town the Money Makers owned, there were Dread banners everywhere, and the streets seemed deserted.

"I can't believe they're still alive," Lightwave scoffed as we walked deeper into the city. I couldn't help but agree, as the death of the Dreads was what all the people in my old city talked about. It was like a dream, being saved by the Warriors. We constantly hoped that the Warriors would take down the Crimson Powers, but it never happened. Well, now it was sort of happening.

Entering the heart of the city, we notice way more banners, and drones of people walking around with tattoos and clothes branding the Dreads. Suddenly, I hear growls behind me, and I turn to see Stinger already transformed into a tiger.

She's about to lunge, but I just manage to pull her back. "What are you doing?" I hiss, "there's no way that we can just walk in there and save the others. We need a plan." Stinger changes back, but she is clearly angry, as if she would charge in at any moment.

"Our main goal is to save the Warriors, and Nova if what Leo said was true. I think our best bet is to keep an eye on them, and wait until they are weakest." Lightwave whispers to the group, and although it's not a great plan, it's better than nothing. However, Stinger shakes her head, and the twins seem wary.

"Right now we have the upper hand. They don't even know we're here! Why risk losing that element of surprise by waiting? This whole city is theirs." Stinger brings up a good point, and the twins agree. However, with this idea, the group is divided.

Luckily, Verity manages to find a compromise by using Lightwave's light energy to make us all invisible. That way, we could still be able to keep track of the Dreads and Crimson Powers, while keeping our element of surprise. Stinger agrees, though seemingly still thirsty for revenge.

Time passes so slowly in the mini-invisible bubble that Lightwave created. As a few of us keep track of what's going on at their base, I suddenly remember what happened to me in the fights against the Money Makers. Instead of turning to a body of water, my body turned to pure fire. I decided to confide in Lightwave, hoping that she knew what was going on.

However, when I told Lightwave, she was confused as well.

"I never knew of someone to have 2 different powers, much less 3. No matter what, though, that makes you one of the strongest people in this group." Then, she leans in and speaks so that only I can hear her: "Our group is inexperienced. Other than Stinger, everyone else doesn't have that much experience. And Verity's powers are kind of useless in battle."

Just as we finish talking, an alarm sounds. In a split second, a group of around ten to twenty walk outside, some wielding weapons. At the very front, I see a person with a hand-shaped scar across his face. Panther. Suddenly, a person probably around my age disappears with someone else. And come back. And disappears with someone else. In a matter of seconds, they're all gone. Who was that? Teleportation? With his back to us, I couldn't tell who it was, but whoever it was must've been powerful. At least we didn't have to fight them.

Lightwave starts to gather all of us, but Stinger's already charging into battle, changing into a panther as she runs into their base. Sighing, Lightwave ran after Stinger, followed by the rest of us. Up ahead, Stinger's already engaging with two people, both of which have powers. Screams echo throughout, and I can see all sorts of powers flying through the air. Even so, I couldn't focus on them as someone collided into me. A lady, wielding bladed knives on both hands. At least she didn't have any powers. I willed myself to turn into fire and threw myself at her, burning her whole body. Her knives clattered to the floor as she screamed in agony. Even with one enemy down, there was no time to waste. We were outnumbered, so I went on to the next enemy.

Super strength. Fireballs. Invisibility. Different super powered individuals were rushing towards me. With my abilities, I was able to take them down. Finally, as the latest person that I fought went down, I saw an opening. The others were still fighting, with Echo even controlling some of the gang members to fight against each other. However, I knew we had to hurry. They just kept coming, and there was no way we could hold for long. Wondering if I still had any other abilities that I didn't figure out, I decided to try and unlock them.

Thinking back to how I unlocked my previous powers, it was all in do-or-die situations. So, I decided to do just that. Looking around, there were still gang members streaming out from deeper inside the base, Dreads or Crimson Powers alike.

As I rushed further inside the base, all sorts of powers were flung at me. But I didn't care. Turning to water, I dodged most attacks, and when that didn't work, I changed to fire. No matter what, I didn't stop running, knowing that we had to win. I willed myself to find any sort of hidden ability that could help me. There was no way we could lose. We had to win for all the Warriors that were lost, for all that was still captured, and above all, for Nye. And, as these thoughts coursed through my brain, light engulfed my surroundings, disintegrating everything in my near vicinity.

"Holy crap," I heard Stinger yell as she was flung back, as well as the gang members near me. Luckily, she wasn't that close to me, and she managed to get up with just a few scratches.

"Sorry," I said sheepishly, but she was laughing.

"Hope, you just got another freaking power!" Looking down, I realized she was right. Now, the tendrils of electricity were where my body was, sending sparks flying. There was no time to marvel, though. There were still people to fight. Just then, I felt power flow through my surroundings, like my power was all around me. Lights started flickering, and as I got closer, it seemed like it was calling for me. As soon as I placed my hand on the light switch on the wall, everything went dark for a second before I felt myself traveling between the electronics. I breathed a sigh of relief. Locating the Warriors now would be a piece of cake.

Chapter. 20

I popped in and out of lights, phones, computers, and more, searching room after room. Most were empty, and the others were just filled with scientists, who all were shocked to see me. However, I didn't stay to chat.

After a few more rooms, I exited out of a lightbulb to enter a huge, open room. In the middle, surrounded by scientists and a few guards, were the Warriors. They were all stuck inside a huge cage, with prison bars that looked like it was made from electricity. The prison felt weird, though, and I couldn't disable it with my electricity. Just then, a few of the scientists saw me, and alerted the guards. Sighing, I went back into the lightbulb, before appearing out of their computers and shocking them. The guards also stood no chance, and I took them out in seconds. After taking out the gang members, I turned back to human form, where the Warriors were cheering. I made out Cypher first, who was shocked that I had similar powers to him, and then Charcoal.

I asked Charcoal if he knew how to get them out, and he

motioned towards a controller near the cage. After pulling the switch, the cage bar's flickered once before turning completely off. All of a sudden, everyone's powers came back, and cheers filled the air. However, there was still a battle outside.

"Guys, Lightwave and the others are still outside, and they need our help!" I shouted over the crowd. There were still some who didn't manage to hear what I just said, but the majority did, and they were already charging out the room, ready to take revenge. The rest soon followed. As Cypher patted me on the back, and Charcoal smiled one of his rare smiles, I knew that we were going to win. They stood no chance now.

Until I realized something. Airless was missing. All of a sudden, I felt my throat seize up. Turning around, I saw Airless, his eyes filled with rage, with malice. But it couldn't be him. Airless didn't have a mohawk. Then, I remembered. Airless had a brother, a twin. Could this be him? As my eyes start to burn, and the effects of zero oxygen start to weigh on me, I turn into a ball of water, and breathe a sigh of relief when I realize that his powers have zero effect on me in this form.

Airless's brother raises his eyebrow, shocked, before he smirks. "Of course, you're Nye's sister. I guess you got two powers, just like him." Nye? He knows Nye?

"What did you do to him?" I say, surprised that I can speak in this form.

"Nothing," he replies, "just sent him on a mission to eliminate the other Warriors roaming free."

I do my best to stop myself from strangling him to death. I needed more answers. "Give the air back, or I'll kill you right now," I threaten, and he shrugs before doing so. As soon as he does, Charcoal and Cypher start wheezing, quickly breathing in the air. "How do you have your brother's powers?" At this, he smiles, crazed, looking just like Eli when he lost Echo.

"I took his power," he laughs, "he left me, so he got what he deserved." What? Airless dead? As I'm about to say something, Charcoal lunges at Airless's brother, managing to grab onto him.

"I will kill you, Casper," Charcoal yells, as Casper starts to scream in pain. Charcoal grips Casper in the face, leaving a similar scar that he gave to Panther. Nevertheless, Casper starts to laugh, his laughs echoing throughout the room.

"It doesn't matter," he chuckles, "as we speak, the other Warriors are slowly losing their air. And I'm the only one who can give it back. So let me go, or all of them die." Charcoal doesn't seem intent on letting go, so I have to pull him back. He looks at me, his eyes full of malice, and I know why. Airless was his best friend. And now he was dead. Even so, there was no way that we could sacrifice all the Warrior's just to avenge Airless's death.

Looking to my right, Cypher nods grimly, silently agreeing to what we had to do.

"There's no other way," I say to Charcoal even as he continues to struggle, "We have to let him go." After a few seconds, Charcoal stops struggling, a look of resignation on his face. Casper chuckles and begins to walk towards the door. Once he left, the three of us rushed out, running through corridors until we found the main clash between the Warriors and the two gangs.

Bodies littered the floor, and more than half who were still fighting were on the floor, gasping for air. Most of the gang members were either running away or lying dead. We all separated, looking around to help any Warriors. As I ran around, I finally found the people who led this rebellion. Stinger was still gasping for air but otherwise seemed fine, and Lightwave was getting to her feet.

As soon as Lightwave sees me, her face lights up. "We saved them," she shouts in glee and I try to act happy, but I can't bring myself to tell Lightwave what happened to Airless. Out of all of us, Charcoal and Lightwave were probably the closest to him, since they were some of the first to get recruited. "What's wrong?" Lightwave asks as she frowns, and she starts to look around.

"Where's Airless?" She asks, and I know I have to tell her the truth.

"He's dead," I mutter, looking down at the floor, "Casper took his powers." In a flash, Lightwave's smile is wiped off and replaced by a frown. Her eyes start to water, before she turns away and walks off.

I feel a hand on my shoulder, and I turn to see Stinger. "Give her some time, Hope. She'll come around." I nod, and Stinger walks off, leaving me alone. As I walk across the field of bodies, I feel a mix of emotions: Exhilaration from the success of this rescue, worry from finding more of my friends dead, and sadness at the lives lost.

From the corner of my eye, I spot Void and Echo. They are both standing over something, their eyes watering. Only when I am closer do I realize what, or who, it is. Verity, her eyes closed and on the floor, with a pool of blood around her. A blade protrudes from her stomach, and her eyes are closed. Verity's death hits me in an instant and I sink to my knees, the shock hitting me like a tidal wave. We've been through so much, and just like that, she's dead.

Verity isn't the only one that was lost. Multi was gone as well, with Boost slumped next to his body, crying. An empty feeling spreads through me, like I just lost everything. Even by saving the Liberti Warriors, we still didn't find Nova, or even my brother, and our leader was dead. It seemed as if all was lost.

Just then, someone appeared. The same person who

disappeared with Panther. The person with teleporting powers. By his side were two others. I shouted a warning to the others near me, and in an instant, they were surrounded.

"Don't move," I warned, bursting into flames. However, the person took off his mask and raised both his hands.

There, unharmed, was Nye. My brother. The two next to him stood up, and I immediately recognized Torch and Ingot.

"We come in peace," Nye managed to say before passing out.

Chapter. 21

I woke up to see Hope standing above me. I was surrounded by dozens of Warriors and dead bodies. The room I was in looked decimated, and everywhere I looked there was some sort of evidence of a superpowered battle.

"Nye, what are you doing here? And how did you teleport?" Hope asks incredulously as she pulls me up.

"I didn't know you guys were here," I responded, "I escaped from the group of Crimson Powers that I was with and took these two captured Warriors back to save Charcoal and the others. We have to hurry, Panther and the others will suspect something when I don't come back and teleport them."

"Let's go," Charcoal shouts over the crowd, "we have to leave before the others come back." Then, Charcoal looks back at me. "Nye, can you teleport us all back to the old Warriors base?" Having mastered my teleportation, I nod and start to send people over. I pop back and forth, sending more and more people, until we're all there.

As soon as we get there, Charcoal is unanimously considered as the new leader, immediately assigning people to new roles and jobs to fix the base. However, Charcoal still gives me a bit of time to catch up with Hope.

As we sit down and share our stories, it feels just like the old times. But better. After a long time, I finally feel free again. Free of the Crimson Powers, free of any gang. I'm a Liberti Warrior.

A year later...

Ever since we took down the Crimson Powers, it's been smooth sailing. Echo and Void immediately passed their training because of their better grasp on powers, and crime was decreasing steadily. Because of Hope's key role in the rescue mission, it wasn't long before she made it into Charcoal's "inner circle". And me? I'm perfectly happy with where I am, being a scout and recruiter for the Warriors. So, in a way, you can say everything's fine.

One day, as I was just going around a nearby city, I heard the screams of a child. With Echo and Shadow, a rookie, we teleported to the noise. However, instead of the usual stopping of a gang, when we got there, nobody was in sight. There was only one message written in fire, carved into the floor.

Beware the Supernova.

The New World

作　　者／Christian D. Chu

出　　版／Christian D. Chu

製作銷售／秀威資訊科技股份有限公司

　　　　　114 台北市內湖區瑞光路76巷69號2樓

　　　　　電話：+886-2-2796-3638

　　　　　傳真：+886-2-2796-1377

網路訂購／秀威書店：https://store.showwe.tw

　　　　　博客來網路書店：https://www.books.com.tw

　　　　　三民網路書店：https://www.m.sanmin.com.tw

　　　　　讀冊生活：https://www.taaze.tw

出版日期／2024年5月

定　　價／300元